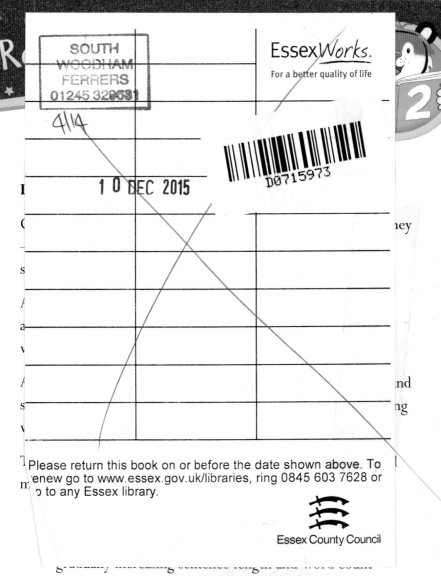
• providing texts that boost a young reader's confidence.

As each book is completed, engaging activities encourage young
readers to look back at the story, while a Picture Dictionary
reinforces new vocabulary. Enjoyment is the key – and reading
together can be great fun for both parent and child!

Prue Goodwin

Lecturer i

1

How to use this series

The **Ready, Steady, Read!** series has 4 levels.
The facing page shows what you can expect to find
in the books at each level.

As your child's confidence grows, they can progress
to books from the higher levels. These will keep them
engaged and encourage new reading skills.

The levels are only meant as guides; together, you and
your child can pick the book that will be just right.

Here are some handy tips for helping children who are
ready for reading!

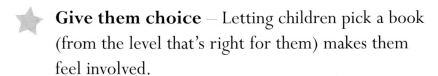

Give them choice – Letting children pick a book
(from the level that's right for them) makes them
feel involved.

Talk about it – Discussing the story and the
pictures helps children engage with the book.

Read it again – Repetition of favourite stories
reinforces learning.

Cheer them on! – Praise and encouragement
builds a child's confidence and the belief in their
growing ability.

LEVEL 1 For first readers

* short, straightforward sentences
* basic, fun vocabulary
* simple, easy-to-follow stories of up to 100 words
* large print and easy-to-read design

LEVEL 2 For developing readers

* longer sentences
* simple vocabulary, introducing new words
* longer stories of up to 200 words
* bold design, to capture readers' interest

LEVEL 3 For more confident readers

* longer sentences with varied structure
* wider vocabulary
* high-interest stories of up to 300 words
* smaller print for experienced readers

LEVEL 4 For able readers

* longer sentences with complex structure
* rich, exciting vocabulary
* complex stories of up to 400 words
* emphasis on text more than illustrations

Once you have read the story, you will find some amazing activities at the back of the book! There are Excellent Exercises for you to complete, plus a super Picture Dictionary.

But first it is time for the story . . .

Ready?

Steady?

Let's read!

Ragnhild Scamell Michael Terry

Ouch!

LITTLE TIGER PRESS
London

Hedgehog was about to
settle down for her
winter sleep . . .

. . . when a red apple landed
   on her back.

"Ouch!" squeaked
         Hedgehog.

"I'll push it off," said Squirrel.

He heaved. And he tugged.

But the apple
stayed put.

Now some of Squirrel's
brown nuts were stuck on
Hedgehog too!

"Try rolling on the grass,"
snorted Pig.

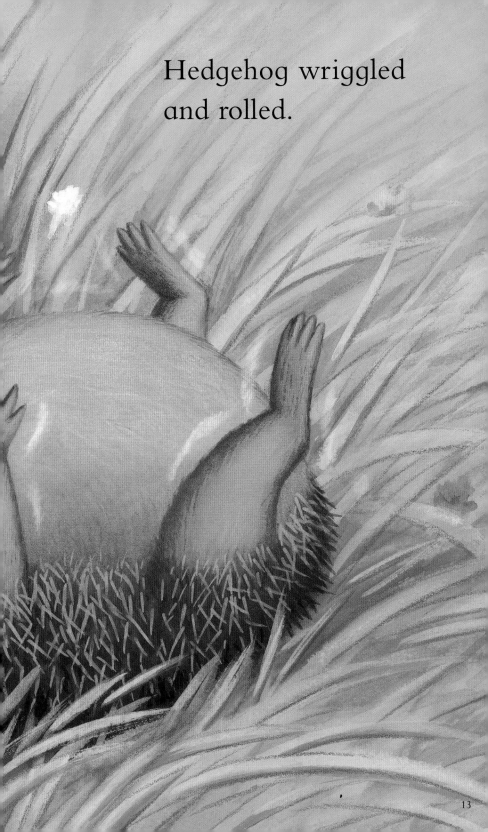

Hedgehog wriggled
and rolled.

But now a green pear
and a crumpled leaf
were on her back too!

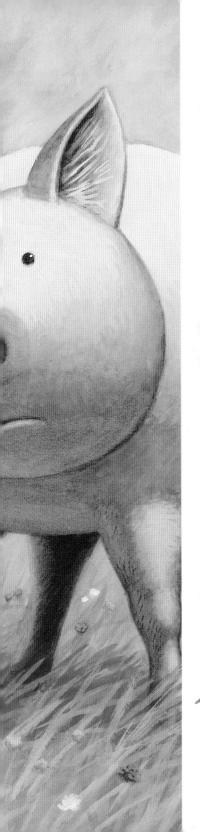

Suddenly, a bit
of blue card
floated down
from the sky . . .

. . . and landed right on
Hedgehog's back.
"It's not fair!"
she cried.

"Wash it all off in the water," croaked Frog.

Splash! But now a pink
water lily was stuck on her
back too!

"Bother!" mumbled Hedgehog. "Squeeze through that hedge," said Pig. "That will brush everything off."

So Hedgehog
squeezed
through.

But now there were
blackberries on her
back too!

"Oooh!" cried Goat.
"You've brought
 LUNCH!"
  "Help yourself!"
said Hedgehog.

So Goat picked off the apple,
the nuts, the pear, the
water lily and the
blackberries. For
pudding, he ate
the card.

"Thank you, Goat!"
cried Hedgehog.

Then she settled in her nest and fell fast asleep.

Excellent Exercises

Have you read the story? Well done! Now it is time for more fun!

Here are some questions about the story. Ask an adult to listen to your answers, and help if you get stuck.

Many Mishaps

In this story, lots of things go wrong for poor Hedgehog. Can you think of a time when something has gone wrong for *you*?

Delicious Dinner

Can you name all the food in this picture? What are *your* favourite things to eat?

Happy Hedgehog

Now describe what Hedgehog is doing in this picture.

Stuck On You

Can you remember how Hedgehog finally gets rid of the things on her back?

Picture Dictionary

Can you read all of these words from the story?

apple

asleep

frog

goat

heaved

hedgehog

leaf

pig

rolled

squirrel

Can you think of any other words that describe these pictures – for example, what colours can you see? Why not try to spell some of these words? Ask an adult to help!

Hopping Mad!

Fred has five frogs. Finn has five frogs, too. And when ten frogs get together, it is party time! But Fred and Finn do not find the froggy madness very funny . . .

Newton

Newton keeps hearing funny noises! "Don't be scared!" he tells his toys. And he sets off in the dark to find out what is making the scary sounds.

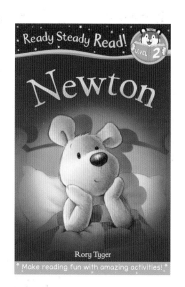

The Wish Cat

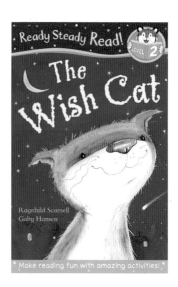

Holly wants a cute little kitten more than anything else in the world. But when she wishes on a star, she ends up with a scruffy cat instead!

Where There's a Bear, There's Trouble!

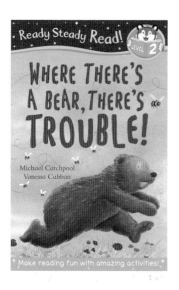

Where there's a bee there's honey. So when Bear spies a bee, he chases after it. But, where there's a bear, there's trouble. So the bee buzzes off as fast as it can . . . !

To Sally, with love – R S
To Mark, from a grateful dad – M T

LITTLE TIGER PRESS, 1 The Coda Centre, 189 Munster Road, London SW6 6AW
First published in Great Britain 2005
This edition published 2013
Text copyright © Ragnhild Scamell 2006, 2013
Illustrations copyright © Michael Terry 2006, 2013
All rights reserved
Printed in China
978-1-84895-670-4
LTP/1800/0591/0413
2 4 6 8 10 9 7 5 3 1

Books in the Series

LEVEL 1 - For first readers

Can't You Sleep, Dotty?

Fred

My Turn!

Rosie's Special Surprise

What Bear Likes Best!

LEVEL 2 - For developing readers

Hopping Mad!

Newton

Ouch!

Where There's a Bear, There's Trouble!

The Wish Cat

LEVEL 3 - For more confident readers

Lazy Ozzie

Little Mouse and the Big Red Apple

Nobody Laughs at a Lion!

Ridiculous!

Who's Been Eating My Porridge?

LEVEL 4 - For able readers

The Biggest Baddest Wolf

Meggie Moon

Mouse, Mole and the Falling Star

The Nutty Nut Chase

Robot Dog